6 Scary

Halloween Stories

for Teens 2:

Urban Legends

PW Pretorius
&
Len du Randt

6 Scary Halloween Stories for Teens 2: Urban Legends is a work of fiction. Names, characters, places, and incidents are either the product of the authors' imagination, or are used fictitiously. Any resemblance to actual persons, living or dead, businesses, companies, events, or locales is entirely coincidental.

For other great titles, visit CLaW Publishing at
www.clawpublishing.com

Serious Warning!

We have it on good authority that anyone reading these stories to a five-year-old will be taken by the Slender Man!

You have been warned!

Stories:

The Clown Statue

"They already ate and bathed, so you just have to tuck them in at nine," Peter said. "And you have both our numbers just in case you need anything."

Melissa nodded. "I'm confident that everything will be fine, Mr. Jones," she said. "You two go have a lovely evening."

"Thanks," Peter said. "And thank you again for being able to sit on such short notice."

"No problem at all," Melissa said. "I love watching the kids."

"Oh, before I forget," Peter said. "There's a bowl of candy for the trick or treatsters, but I don't want Amy and John to go out themselves. They're too young for it, and we can consider perhaps doing something next year."

"No problem at all, sir," Melissa said and waved to Peter and his wife as they got into their car and drove off.

After handing out candy to a few trick or treatsters, Melissa got the kids to bed and tucked them in. She read them a bed time story and then switched off the lights. "Piece of cake," she said and made her way to the kitchen. "Easiest money, ever."

RING!

Melissa let out a shriek and jumped a little when the phone next to the fridge suddenly let out a shrill ring.

"Hello?" she asked.

"Hello, Melissa, it's me, Peter."

"Oh, hi, Mr. Jones."

"I'm just calling to check in and make sure that everything's okay? Are the kids in bed yet?"

"Just tucked them in, yes. They were wonderful, as always."

"Fantastic! We're going to be another two hours or so, and then we'll be there. Please help yourself to anything in the fridge, and feel free to watch a movie or something."

"Will do, Mr. Jones. Thanks again."

After making herself a snack, Melissa called her best friend, Sally, and chatted for a few minutes. Then she spent another half an hour chatting to her boyfriend. Finally, she made her way to the living room and switched on the television.

"Mary, get out of the house! Jack the maniac is—"

Melissa switched to another channel.

"It's not enough to just kill these things, Sarge! You've got to *kill them dead!*"

Melissa rolled her eyes. "Well this just sucks," she said and sunk down on the couch. Every channel had some or other horror movie playing, and she would much rather prefer a romantic comedy on a night like this.

It was while flipping channels that she first noticed the life-sized statue of the clown standing in the corner of the room.

"Geez dude," Melissa said and approached the statue. "You almost gave me a heart attack."

The statue just stood there, motionless. In the low light and with the tense music coming from the television, the statue sent a shiver crawling down Melissa's spine.

Melissa sat back down, but no matter how much she tried to focus on the television and ignore the clown, she couldn't shake the feeling that the thing was looking at her, watching her every move. Finally, she got up from the couch and made her way to the kitchen where she dialed Peter's number.

"Hi Melissa, is everything okay?"

"Everything's fine, Mr. Jones," Melissa said. "I just quickly called to ask for your permission..."

"My permission? To do what...?"

"To throw a blanket over that clown statue you have in the living room. I know it's just my imagination, but it feels like it's watching me, and it's kinda creeping me out."

"Melissa," Peter said. "I want you to listen to me very carefully, okay?"

"Okay...?"

"I want you to go up and get the kids from their beds. Then I want you to run over to the neighbors and call the police. Can you do that?"

"I... I guess I can. But why?"

"Because," Peter said. "We don't have a clown statue!"

The Samaritan

Sue's feet were killing her. She spent the better part of the morning in the mall, walking up and down stores as she did her monthly shopping. The sun stung her eyes as she left the mall, and she had to take a minute to remember where she had parked her car.

"Oh there you are," she said softly as she pushed the shopping cart towards her blue car in the distance.

When she finally got to her car, it took another five minutes to unpack everything into her trunk. She was about to close the trunk when a young man approached her.

"Excuse me, ma'am," the man said and smiled broadly. He was wearing a suit and tie, and had a briefcase in his hand. "But I couldn't help noticing the flat tire you've got there."

"Oh dear," Sue said and walked around the car to where the young man was pointing. The tire was indeed flat, and needed to be changed.

"Can I give you a hand with that?" the young man offered.

"That would be mighty sweet of you, thanks," Sue said.

"Think nothing of it," he said and placed his briefcase and jacket in the trunk. He then took out the spare wheel, jack and wheel spanner and proceeded to change her tire.

"You are too kind," Sue said and held out a dollar note to the young man.

He merely laughed and held up his hands. "I can't take your money," he said. "But I tell you what. If you could drive me to the other side of the mall where my car is parked, I'd be most grateful."

"That sounds fair enough," said Sue. She closed the trunk and was about to unlock her door when she wondered out loud, "What are you doing on this side of the mall?"

The man looked at her and frowned. "Excuse me?" he asked.

"Well, it doesn't look like you've been shopping all morning, so I just wondered what brought you to this side of the mall?"

He smiled and raked his fingers through his neatly combed hair. "I... erm... I met up with a few friends of mine. I walked them to their car to see them off, and ran into you on my way back."

Sue wanted to believe the strapping young lad who so eagerly helped her change her flat tire, but something gnawed at her gut. She couldn't put her finger on it, but something made her hesitant about letting this kind man get into her car.

She was about to open the door when it struck her.

The flat tire!

It wasn't deflated... it was slashed!

"Oh dear," she said. "I forgot something at the last store I visited."

"Should I go and get it for you?" the young man offered.

"No need," she said. "I know exactly where I left it, and it would go quicker if I went to go and get it than to try and explain."

"No problem at all," the young man said. "I'll wait here for you."

"Wonderful," said Sue. "I'll be right back."

Sue then made her way to the mall, only looking back every now and again to make sure that the young man was still waiting at her car. Once inside the mall, she headed straight to the nearest security guard and told him what had happened.

"Please take me to this man," the guard said, and Sue led him back to her car.

When they got there, however, there was no sign of the man anywhere. Sue opened the trunk to show the guard the man's jacket and briefcase. The guard opened the briefcase and gasped.

"What's wrong?" Sue asked.

He didn't answer, but instead, turned the briefcase towards her. Inside was a pair of gloves, rope, duct tape, and a sharp butcher's knife.

Slender Man

"Come on, Dylan," Stacey urged. "We're going to be late!"

"I'm walking as fast as I can," Dylan said. "My legs are aching."

Stacey stopped at a rusted metal gate and waited for Dylan to catch up.

She looked down the street and then tried the gate.

It opened with a loud squeak.

"What are you doing?" Dylan asked when he finally caught up with Stacey.

"If we go through here," she said, "we skip that entire section up ahead. We'd then be on time."

"Are you insane?" Dylan shrieked. "Have you completely lost your mind?"

"It's just a short cut through the park, Dylan," Stacey said. "Why are you being such a girl about it?"

"Haven't you heard about the Slender Man and how he got that group of kids that walked through here last year on Halloween? They were never heard from or seen again!"

Stacey laughed out loud. "Don't tell me you actually believe that story?"

"It's not a story, Stacey, the Slender Man is real, and he got those kids, I tell you."

"Okay," she said, "Let's assume that he's real—"

"He *is* real!"

Stacey ignored him. "Let's assume for a minute that you're right and he is real," she said, "doesn't the rumor say that he'll only catch you if you've been naughty?"

"I... I guess..."

"And...? Have you been naughty today?"

Dylan didn't answer her. He just stared at the footpath that led into the darkness of the park."

"Come," Stacey said and pulled Dylan by the arm. "We're wasting time debating this."

"But... but..." Dylan tried to say, but Stacey ignored him.

They were halfway through the park, surrounded by total darkness when they first smelled something foul. As they walked, the strong odor intensified, and eventually they both struggled to breathe.

"What's that smell?" Dylan asked.

"I don't know," Stacey said and looked around to see if she could locate the source of the terrible smell.

"There!" Dylan cried out and pointed to a cluster of trees.

Between the trees, the two children could clearly see the outline of a tall figure dressed entirely in black. They couldn't see any features on its face, but could hear a low growling sound coming from the figure.

"It's the Slender Man!" Dylan said. He wanted to get away from there as quickly as he could.

"Nonsense," Stacey said. "The Slender Man doesn't exist! Even if it did, we didn't do anything wrong, so it'll leave us alone."

The figure started advancing towards them, the smell intensifying even more with each long stride it took.

"It's coming for us!" Dylan said. "*We have to run!*"

"We didn't do anything wrong," Stacey said. "He can't hurt us!"

"You know that money we used to buy our Halloween costumes with?"

"Yes...?"

"Well, I stole it from mom's purse!"

"What?"

"You told me to!"

"I was kidding. I only made a joke!"

"How was I supposed to know that?"

Stacey didn't have a chance to answer.

The slender, faceless figure roared like a lion as it leapt towards both children.

The Psychic

"And that was a classic by Barbra Streisand," the DJ announced on the radio. "We have some Nickelback coming up next, but first, we have an anonymous, self-proclaimed psychic on the line that would like to share a few words with us."

Lightning flashed outside, and David activated the wipers to clear the windshield from the few drops that had begun dripping down.

"Hello? a woman's voice spoke from the radio. "Is this the Carsten's Show?"

"That's it, anonymous," the DJ confirmed. "You're speaking to Rick."

"Oh, hi Rick," the voice greeted. "Is this live?"

"You're on the air, yes."

"Fantastic!"

"You said that you had an important message or vision that you had to share with our listeners?"

"I do, yes," the woman said. "I received a divine warning, and hope that your listeners would heed to the prediction that I'm about to share with you."

"Okay, but before you do, you said that you're a psychic, right?"

"I'm a medium," she said, "but I do have the gift of second sight."

"Right," the DJ said, and David smirked at the condescending tone in the radio personality's voice. "Now tell us more about this vision or whatever you had?"

"Death," the woman said, "and lots of it."

"Could you be any more specific?"

"The vision comes in bits and pieces," she said, "sometimes in visible images, and sometimes in feelings. I sense that there will be a brutal massacre tonight, at a gathering of people."

"Lady, it's Halloween, everyone will be out partying or gathering in groups somewhere or another."

"This is different," the woman said. "It's not at a house or something. As far as I can tell, it's as some or other academic institution."

"Like a school?"

"Correct, it could be a school, or a college campus. I'm not sure."

"So what do you think is going to happen at this school gathering?"

"I'm not sure, but all I see is an axe and a lot of blood. I can hear screaming, but can't see individual faces or anything."

"Interesting," the DJ said. "We'll continue this discussion right after a few words from our sponsors."

David pulled his car into a gas station and filled it up. A storm was coming. He was glad that he had a rain coat in his trunk.

"Would that be all?" the shop attendant asked when David paid for the fuel.

David nodded, shoved the change into his pocket, and left without saying a word. He then got back into the car, and drove off into the darkness of night.

"We're back," Rick, the radio DJ said. "And on the line with us again is the psychic medium who would prefer to remain anonymous. You there, anonymous?"

"I am," she confirmed.

"Okay, so to bring new listeners up to speed, you claim that you have some sort of prediction about a massacre at some or other school function, right?"

"Correct."

"And how can you be so certain that it's going to happen tonight? Did you receive a date and time with your premonition?"

"Not as blatantly as some of the images I see, no," she answered.

"So this could happen next week, or year, or might even have happened in the past?"

"No," she said. "The feeling I get about the visions are current... something that has to happen today."

"In this country?"

"Correct," the voice said. "Always within twenty miles from where I am."

"And you're in town, right?"

"I am, yes."

"Hot dang! Well, there you have it, listeners," the DJ said. "So if you're out partying tonight, stay away from schools, or the Boogeyman's gonna getcha."

"That's not entirely what I meant—"

David snapped off the radio and pulled his car over to the side of the road. He got out and briskly walked around to the trunk. Inside, he removed his raincoat and donned it after which he then removed a large double-headed axe. He looked up at the School's wide open gate just as lightning flashed overhead and then proceeded towards the sound of loud music while dragging his axe behind him.

The Initiation

The dark road twisted and snaked through the mountain pass, and Sandy had to focus to make sure that she didn't veer off the shoulder of the road. She hated driving here late at night and wished that they would erect street lamps or something that would at least light up the roads somewhat.

"Hey love," she answered her phone when it vibrated in her pocket. "I'm almost there."

She turned down the volume of her radio.

"It went really well," she said. "You won't believe what Tom paid for the band alone."

After a few more minutes, the battery died. She sighed as she returned the cell back to her pocket, and then rolled down the window for some much needed fresh air.

Sandy was always nervous when it came to this stretch of road, especially on Halloween. She tried to keep her thoughts positive by thinking about the office party she had just attended.

"Thanks again for helping out with all the arrangements," Tom said when the party was over and she was about to leave. "I really appreciate it."

"No problem at all," she lied. It took a lot of favors and small miracles to get everything running without a hitch. She only did it to prove that she could handle larger projects and thus get the promotion she'd been shooting for over the last six months.

"Are you going through the city?" Tom asked her.

"No, I really just want to get home as quickly as possible, so I'm taking the shorter route through the mountain pass."

"At Devil's Knuckles?"

She chuckled and nodded.

"Drive extra safe, please," he urged. "There's a rumor that on Halloween, gangs drive there without their lights on. When the driver flashes his or her lights to point this out, they then follow the driver and kill him or her as part of a brutal gang initiation."

"That's an urban legend," Sandy said and laughed. "We all know it's not true."

"Well, stay safe anyway, okay?"

Sandy agreed, but knew that she had nothing to worry about.

She turned the volume of the radio back up, and when she looked up, a black mass was almost right on top of her. She activated her brights to see what it was, and her heart skipped a beat when she realized it was a car without its headlights on that just drove past her. When switching over to brights, it might have appeared as if she had been flashing her lights to the driver of the other car.

"It's just an urban legend," she whispered to try and calm her nerves, but when she checked the rear view mirror, her heart sank when she saw the car turning around and starting to follow her.

The car gained speed until it was almost upon her, and then started flashing its lights.

"No, no, no!" Sue cried out and tried to speed up in an attempt to shake her pursuer.

She had no such luck.

The car behind her kept flashing its lights and then started honking its horn at her as well.

"*Leave me alone!*"

The car relentlessly pursued, and when they arrived at a straight stretch in the road, the car overtook her and then suddenly braked hard.

Sandy slammed down on her brakes, and her car came to a complete stop with a hard jerk.

"What do you want from me?" she screamed at the car in front of her. She wanted to call her husband, but then remembered that her phone's battery had died. The driver's door of the car in front of her opened, and she could see the silhouette of someone getting out and limping towards her.

"I... I've called the police!" she shouted, hoping that it would deter the person from coming any closer.

Knock, knock, knock!

Someone knocked on her window! Sandy moved only her eyes and saw that it was a man with scruffy, long hair and dirty overalls.

Sandy did her best to ignore him, but after the knocking continued for some time, she opened her window just a fraction. "What do you want from me?" she cried out in despair.

"I-I-I... whu-whu-whu-you m-m-m-must c-c-c-come with muh-muh-me," the man said in a stutter.

"I'll do no such thing," Sandy said. "Please leave me alone! I've called the police, and they're on their way, so you best get out of here while you still can!"

"Puh-puh-puh-please cuh-cuh-come wuh-wut... Please g-g-g-get out of your cuh-cuh-cuh-car lady!"

"Please leave," Sandy sobbed. "Please just leave..."

"Thu-thu-thu-there--"

"*Leave me alone!*" she screamed and stepped down on the gas pedal. She almost ran the man over and narrowly missed his car in her desperate attempt to escape from this weirdo.

"Puh-please lady!" the man called out after her. "Thu-thu-there's a m-m-m-man wuh-wu-with an axe huh-hiding in your b-b-b-back seat!"

The Chain Letter

James was getting ready for the Halloween party when he decided to check his e-mails one last time. A new mail arrived from someone named Teddy, and at first, James was reluctant to open it. What changed his mind was the subject that read, "Do this, or die!"

"Oh brother," James said and rolled his eyes. "It's another one of those chain letters."

He would normally just delete mails like these, but he was on his way to a Halloween party and figured that it might just put him in the right morbid mood for the evening. "Let's see what you have to say," he whispered and clicked on the mail.

It read:
Hi there!

My name is Teddy. I am 17 years old. I have no eyes, and have blood all over my face. I've been killed by a girl called Monica. She was jealous of me and stabbed out my eyes and pushed me down a flight of stairs. If you do not forward this mail to 25 people saying "Monica did it!" I will hide under your bed tonight and will stab out your eyes.

Don't believe me?

Peter Stevenson got this mail and didn't forward it to a single person. I stabbed out his eyes and he bled to death on his bed. Ha ha ha ha! Do you want that to happen to you?

George Mason sent the mail out, but only to ten people. Not good enough, George! Believe it or not, George is now in a coma, and they don't think he'll ever come out of it. Ha ha ha!

Derick Dicky was smart! He sent out the mail to all 25 people and later that day, he picked up a $100 bill on the sidewalk. He was also promoted to head engineer at the company he worked for, and his girlfriend agreed to marry him. He and his wife are now living happily ever after and have two beautiful children.

Send the mail within the next five minutes, or face the consequences!

Sincerely,
Teddy

    James rolled his eyes and laughed out loud. He had read many letters like these, but this one was by far the most outrageous. He couldn't wait to tell the others about it, and clicked on DELETE before shutting down his computer.

"Be safe, dear, and be back before ten!"

"Okay mom," James said and headed out to the party.

Everything went great, and James even got a kiss on the cheek from Monique, his long-time crush. All-in-all, it was the perfect evening.

"Did you enjoy the party?" James's mother asked when he returned home.

"It was awesome, mom," James said and grabbed a quick snack before heading to bed. He kept thinking about the e-mail that he received from Teddy, and chuckled at how stupid it was. He reminded himself to write his own version in the morning and send it out to a few of his friends to freak them out.

"Stupid mail," James said and chuckled. He rolled onto his side and fell asleep.

A few hours later, James woke up. Something was bothering him, but he couldn't put his finger on it.

Everything in the room was engulfed in darkness, so he couldn't see anything, but it was what he heard that freaked him out. He heard heavy breathing right next to him.

"Who... who's there?" James asked with a coarse voice.

No answer but the heavy breathing.

James turned around to switch on the bed lamp, and squinted when light flooded the room. He breathed out a sigh of relief, and when he turned to see what was creating the breathing noise, he only had a brief glimpse of the blood soaked face with its hollowed out eye sockets before everything went black.

*   *   *

Did you enjoy this book?
If so, please take a minute to leave us a review on Amazon.com

If you liked *6 Scary Halloween Stories for Teens 2: Urban Legends,* you will **love** *The Gobbler*, also by PW Pretorius and Len du Randt:

Grab this exciting title at http://www.killthemdead.net today!

Manufactured by Amazon.ca
Bolton, ON